MCFL Distribution Center Children's
J Fiction Alter
A new arrival :
31111037797840

W9-BZU-452

9-16

ALSO BY ANNA ALTER

Sprout Street Neighbors: Five Stories

A Photo for Greta

Disappearing Desmond

Abigail Spells

SPROUT STREET
NEIGHBORS

A New Arrival

BOOK 2

ANNA ALTER

ALFRED A. KNOPF NEW YORK

THIS IS A BORZOI BOOK PUBLISHED BY ALFRED A. KNOPF

This is a work of fiction. Names, characters, places, and incidents either are the product of the author's imagination or are used fictitiously. Any resemblance to actual persons, living or dead, events, or locales is entirely coincidental.

Copyright © 2016 by Anna Alter

All rights reserved. Published in the United States by Alfred A. Knopf, an imprint of Random House Children's Books, a division of Penguin Random House LLC, New York.

Knopf, Borzoi Books, and the colophon are registered trademarks of Penguin Random House LLC.

Visit us on the Web! randomhousekids.com

Educators and librarians, for a variety of teaching tools, visit us at RHTeachersLibrarians.com

Library of Congress Cataloging-in-Publication Data
Alter, Anna. —
A new arrival / Anna Alter. — First edition.
pages cm. — (Sprout Street neighbors ; [2])
Summary: The animals who live in the apartment building on Sprout Street have a new neighbor, Mili, who just moved in from Hawaii.
ISBN 978-0-385-75562-7 (trade) — ISBN 978-0-385-75563-4 (lib. bdg.) — ISBN 978-0-385-75565-8 (ebook)
[1. Friendship—Fiction. 2. Neighbors—Fiction. 3. Apartment houses—Fiction. 4. Animals—Fiction.] I. Title.
PZ7.A4635Ne 2016
[Fic]—dc23
2014048941

The text of this book is set in 14-point Perrywood.
The illustrations were created using pen and ink with acrylic.

Printed in the United States of America
January 2016
10 9 8 7 6 5 4 3 2 1

First Edition

Random House Children's Books supports the First Amendment and celebrates the right to read.

For my little Hugo

CONTENTS

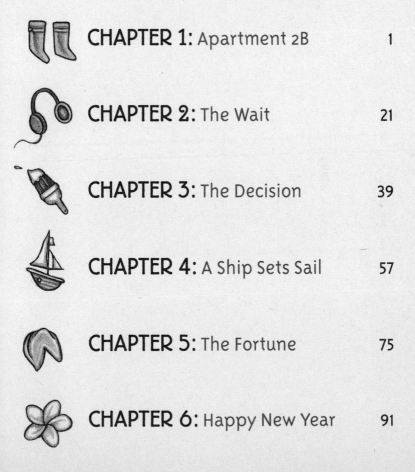

A New Arrival

CHAPTER 1

Apartment 2B

The sky poured rain onto 24 Sprout Street. Violet sat on the porch swing and reached into her basket. "This will do nicely," she said, picking up a ball of yellow wool. The swing rocked back and forth. She listened to the rain pitter-patter on the roof, then splash down onto the azalea bushes.

Screeeeeech! Violet jumped, falling out of her seat. She walked to the stoop to see what was making such a terrible noise. A truck pulled close to the sidewalk and stopped in front of the building.

Just then, the wind picked up and sprayed water on Violet's feet. A chill climbed up her back and made her feathers stand on end. *"Ah-CHOO!"* Violet sneezed.

A small figure got out of the truck and opened a large umbrella. Violet squinted her eyes. All she could see of the stranger was a yellow raincoat and a pair of green galoshes.

"Ah-CHOO!" Violet sneezed again.

She was getting drenched, so she picked up her knitting and went inside. On the landing she found Henry, sitting on a step and muttering to himself.

"Hi, Hen— *Ah-CHOO!*"
sneezed Violet.

"There you are!" said
Henry. "I was just coming to
see you. I need your help.
My trench coat has a tear
and needs mending."

Everyone at 24 Sprout Street
depended on Violet to mend their clothes. It
seemed there was nothing she couldn't fix.

"Of course," she said, stepping toward him,
ker-splish ker-splosh. She looked down. "Perhaps
I better just change my clothes first."

Once inside her apartment, Violet put on a
dry sweater, a skirt, and some wool socks.

"*Ah-CHOO!*" she sneezed.

When she took out her hankie to blow her
nose, it felt as if her head was spinning. She

grabbed on to a kitchen chair to get her balance, then wobbled into the hallway to look for Henry.

Leaning over the railing, she peered down the steps. In front of apartment 2B, directly across from Emma's, was a pair of green galoshes, shiny with raindrops. No one had lived in that apartment for so long, Violet had almost forgotten it was there.

If she was going to have a new neighbor, a warm welcome was in order. Violet went back inside her apartment and pulled out a piece of paper. She picked up a marker and wrote *WEL-COME* in big red letters across the top. Underneath it, she drew a picture of the oak tree in the yard, filled with leaves and acorns. At the bottom, she signed her name.

Violet gazed at her work of art and began to imagine what the new neighbor would be like. Maybe she would like to write poetry, like Henry, or plant rosebushes, like Wilbur?

There was a knock at the door. Before she could answer, Emma burst through with her paws in the air.

"Violet! Did you HEAR? I have a new neighbor. WE have a new neighbor. She is moving in downstairs as we speak!"

"Yes," said Violet. "I saw her galoshes."

"We should go welcome her, don't you think? Yes, yes, we should. Let's go now!"

"*Ah-CHOO!*" said Violet. "Yes, let's." She

put her drawing in her pocket and walked downstairs with Emma, who knocked at apartment 2B.

At first, there was no answer. But then they heard the *slush-slush-slide* of boxes being pushed along the floor. Slowly, the doorknob turned. The door opened just enough for a pointy nose to peek through and give a sniff.

"Hello!" said Emma. "We are your new neighbors, Emma and Violet. We've come to welcome you to the building!"

The nose went back inside. Then the door opened wide and a face appeared around it. Two round eyes blinked from beneath a fancy blue beret. The new neighbor reached up to slide the hat off her head, and her mouth curled into a smile.

"Thank you," she giggled. "My name is Mililani, but you can call me Mili. Please come in!"

Emma and Violet followed Mili into her living room, filled with boxes piled to the ceiling. They looked like cardboard skyscrapers. In the middle of the room was a metal bin holding a stack of framed pictures.

"What's in here?" Violet asked.

"Those are my paintings," said Mili.

"I am something of an artist myself," said Violet, perking up. "May I see?"

"Sure," said Mili, walking to the bin and pulling a painting out from the middle of the stack. It was a picture of a rocky beach surrounded by palm trees. The sky above was a brilliant blue. In the distance, a volcano sent smoke winding up into the soft, feathery clouds. It looked so real, you could almost reach out and touch it.

Emma's jaw dropped. "You are so talented! Isn't she talented, Violet?"

Violet's eyes got wide and her cheeks turned pink. She felt a tiny pinch in her stomach. "It's very nice," she peeped.

"Thanks," said Mili. "It's a picture of the view from my old apartment in Hawaii."

Violet reached into her pocket and wrapped

her wing around her drawing, squeezing it into a little crumpled ball. She cleared her throat.

"I'm afraid I'm a little under the weather today. I'll have to join you another time. Welcome to the building, Mili." She rushed out the door.

Hurrying through the hallway, Violet couldn't bring herself to look up from her feet, until—*THUD*— she crashed into something and lifted her eyes.

"Oh! I'm sorry, Henry! I didn't see you there!" she cried.

"That's all right, I suppose." Henry made a big show of pulling himself up off the floor.

"I'm glad we ran into each other." She smiled. "You can give me your trench coat to mend."

"Never mind about that," said Henry. "I met our new neighbor and she offered to do it."

Violet's stomach pinched again. "Well, good. Good. I have to go now, Henry. I'm not feeling so grea— *Ah-CHOO!*"

Henry jumped back. "Don't let me keep you!"

Violet slunk back to her apartment. She had never been more embarrassed. *"Ah-CHOO!"* she sneezed. The room seemed to sway and Violet's knees felt weak. She went straight to bed.

That night, she had strange dreams. Waking with a start, she looked out the window. The sky was clear and the moon cast long shadows on the lawn, making the oak tree look twice its size. She closed her eyes and went back to sleep.

"Hel-LO!" Emma shouted as she burst through Violet's front door. "Anybody home?"

Violet blinked. The bright sunbeams coming in her window took her by surprise.

"Good afternoon! How are you feeling?" asked Emma, carrying a tray into the room.

"Is it afternoon?" Violet asked, jumping to her feet. But they were not steady and the room began to spin. She sank back down 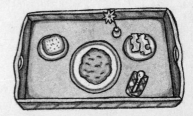 onto her bed. "Still a little under the weather, I guess," she confessed.

"I brought lunch!" cried Emma, handing her

the tray. It held a bowl of lentil soup, rye toast, and two slices of Swiss cheese. Having skipped dinner the night before, Violet was quite hungry.

"Don't forget dessert," squeaked an unfamiliar voice. Mili popped into the room and put a basket of macaroons on the bedside table.

"Oh, hi, Mili," said Violet, taking a spoonful of her soup.

"I hope you are feeling better," Mili added.

Violet put down her spoon and looked up at Emma. Around her neck was the kerchief Violet had made her for her birthday. Violet straightened up a little. "Thank you for lunch."

"You should get some rest," Emma said firmly, turning to go. Mili followed her out of the room. Violet set the tray aside, then lay back in bed and closed her eyes.

A loud knock at the door woke her. She had just enough time to sit up again before Fernando and Wilbur peered in.

"Violet," said Fernando, "Emma told us you were sick! Here, I brought you something."

He reached into a canvas bag embroidered with his initials. Violet had sewn it for him last year. He pulled out a thermos of hot lemon tea. "To clear your head," he said.

Wilbur was holding something behind his back. When he brought his paws around, a bouquet of mari-golds lit up the room. They sat proudly in a vase that Violet had made for him in her pottery class.

"You can borrow it," he said, "until you're feeling better." Wilbur set down the flowers. Then he and Fernando made their way out.

Violet reached for some tea. She looked at the bouquet and remembered how the vase always sat in Wilbur's window, filled with flowers from his garden.

There was another knock. This time, it was Henry.

"Violet! Are you still sick? Oh, you are. I do feel terrible. I wish I hadn't been so gruff yesterday. I am sorry. Here, I brought you something." He reached into his pocket and placed an envelope on Violet's lap. She opened it and pulled out a card with a portrait of Violet on the front. The card said, *Get well soon!*

"I'm not the great artist that you are," he added, "but I wanted to make you something."

"Thank you, Henry. I am already feeling much better," said Violet.

Henry closed the door behind him, and Violet settled in to rest at last. She looked at the things on her bed stand, and a feeling of happiness came over her. She picked up one of Mili's cookies and took a bite. Then she closed her eyes and slept all the way until the next morning.

When she woke up, she hopped out of bed and headed downstairs, straight to Mili's apartment.

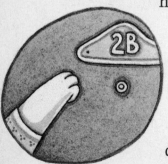

"Hello," said Mili.

"Thank you for the cookies," said Violet. "I'm sorry I didn't say that yesterday."

"That's all right," said Mili. "Would you like to come in?"

Violet was surprised at
how different Mili's apartment looked. She had un-
packed three shelves full of
books, two sets of dishes,
and several chairs. There

were a number of paintings hanging on the
wall above the fireplace. And there, next to the
window, was Violet's drawing, the one she had
made for Mili. The wrinkles had been smoothed
out, and it had been placed in a polished silver
frame.

Mili saw the look of surprise on Violet's face.
"I hope you don't mind! I found it in the hallway
yesterday. I thought it looked like a Picasso!"

"Thank you," Violet said, blushing.

Violet and Mili spent the rest of the morning
among the boxes, chatting about their favorite

places to paint and the best kind of watercolor brushes.

When she got up to go, she looked at Mili. "Welcome to the building," she said. This time, she meant it, inside and out.

CHAPTER 2

The Wait

Emma leapt out of bed, made breakfast for two, and packed it up to bring across the hall. Sunlight sparkled through the windows and danced across the floor. She couldn't wait to visit apartment 2B. Having a new neighbor was like getting a big, shiny present every day of the week.

Emma swung her front door open and skipped through. She hadn't missed a breakfast with Mili since her arrival at 24 Sprout Street. Today, Emma held a bowl of clementines, two

buttered English muf-
fins, hard-boiled eggs,
and a pot of steaming
hot chocolate.

She trotted to her new neighbor's door and
raised her paw to knock, *tuk-tok*. Then she
stepped back and waited. But nothing happened.
It was quiet in apartment 2B.

"That's odd," thought Emma. "Mili doesn't
usually go out this early." Emma set the clementines down next to the doormat and went back
to her apartment.

She paced back and forth, walking and thinking, thinking and walking. "Why would Mili go
out before breakfast? And more important, why
wouldn't she tell ME first?" She took a bite of a
hard-boiled egg.

Then an idea popped into her head. "Perhaps Mili is planning a surprise for me!" The more Emma thought about it, the more it made sense. "That would explain everything," thought Emma. "She must be picking up supplies."

Emma finished her egg and skipped to her closet. "I should wear something special for the occasion," she thought. So she pulled out a red blouse with silk roses around the col- lar. She put it on and looked in the mirror. "Per- fect," she said out loud.

Emma bounced into the hallway and perched on the steps to wait. She didn't know what she was waiting for, but it was bound to be fantastic. Surprises always were.

Klip-klop, klip-klop. Someone was coming up the steps. Emma got ready. She closed her eyes and smiled wide.

The steps slowed, then stopped in front of her. It was quiet for a moment. Emma opened one eye to take a peek. There stood Wilbur, holding his gardening gloves.

"Morning, Emma," said Wilbur. "What is it you're doing?"

"Oh, hi, Wilbur," said Emma. "I'm just waiting for Mili. She is going to give me a surprise."

"I love surprises," said Wilbur. "Do you mind if I wait with you?"

"Sure," sang Emma. Surprises were even better with two. Emma and Wilbur waited patiently, but no one came.

"When will Mili arrive?" asked Wilbur.

"I'm not sure," said Emma. "Any moment, probably." The longer they waited, the more excited she became. "She may be picking up an ice cream cake or renting a marching band. You never know with Mili!"

After a while, Wilbur stood up. "I should get back to work," he said. "If Mili brings a marching band, come and get me!"

Emma nodded and folded her paws on her

lap. She wiggled her shoulders. She tapped her toes. Finally, she could sit no longer. She hopped up and returned to her apartment.

She paced around some more, then glanced at the clock. It was nearly lunchtime. She made a tall pitcher of iced blackberry tea and poured some into a Mason jar. Then she bounded out the door, hopeful Mili would have returned by now with the surprise, whatever it was.

She marched across the hall and raised her paw. She knocked firmly on Mili's door, *tuk-tok-TOK*. Still, it was quiet.

Emma sighed. This surprise sure was taking a long time. She set the tea down by the door and spun around, nearly knocking over Fernando.

"Afternoon, Emma!" chuckled Fernando, reaching for the stair railing to steady himself.

"Hi, Fernando," she said.

Emma stopped and thought for a moment. Then another idea popped into her head. "Do you want to come with me to meet Mili at Sweetcakes?" she asked. "She is going to give me a surprise there."

"Sure," said Fernando. "I could use a blueberry muffin."

"Great!" said Emma as they headed downstairs. "She's probably buying me croissants as we speak. She knows I love them."

"I love them, too," said Fernando, thinking of changing his order from a blueberry muffin.

They headed down Sprout Street toward Sweetcakes. When they arrived, Emma twirled through the door and into the middle of the store. She hopped to a stop and looked around. Everything was still. The tables were empty. Emma got a sudden sinking feeling. She walked up to the counter and rang the bell.

"Excuse me," she said when the baker's assistant arrived, "have you seen anyone in here today buying croissants?"

The assistant furrowed her brow. "I'm sorry, I haven't. We've only had one customer

all day. Ms. Bunkerstein came in for a loaf of pumpernickel."

Emma turned around and looked at Fernando, and then the floor. "I don't think I'm hungry anymore," she said quietly. For the first time that day, Emma was not in the mood for a surprise.

"But we just got here." Fernando frowned.

"I know," said Emma, heading toward the door.

Fernando went to the counter and ordered a chocolate croissant to go. Then he ran to catch up with Emma, who was walking quickly back to 24 Sprout Street. "Maybe Mili will give you the surprise tomorrow?" he said, a little out of breath.

But Emma wasn't listening. She walked with her paws in her pockets and looked at the ground.

She arrived at her apartment in a very serious mood. Emma never felt serious. It didn't suit her. She just couldn't understand what was taking so long. Waiting didn't suit her, either.

The next morning, Emma opened her door a crack and peered across the hall. Then she went back into her kitchen and piled a large stack of cheese blintzes on a tray. One for every day Mili had been her neighbor.

She swung into the hallway, her blintzes bouncing cheerfully up and down. Today was a great day for a surprise.

She lifted her paw to knock. Apartment 2B was silent. Emma sighed.

But then she heard something. *Pit-a-pat.* She froze. Then she knocked again, this time as hard as she could, *ba-BANG*.

There was a little shuffling, then quiet. Emma waited, her heart thumping. She knocked a third time, *BANG BANG*. Then she heard slow, steady footsteps. The handle turned and the door opened.

Mili looked at Emma, then pulled a large set of headphones off her ears. "Hi, Emma! I almost didn't hear you knock. Did you bring me clementines yesterday, and some tea?"

"Yes, that was me," said Emma, waiting patiently for Mili to move aside and let her in. When she did, Emma followed her closely, looking around for ribbons or

confetti. But everything seemed just as it usually was. They went into the kitchen.

Mili placed her headphones on the table. Emma set her tray next to them and sat down. Mili sat down, too.

"I'm so glad you're home at last," Emma began, plopping her paws on her lap. "Breakfast just wasn't the same without you." Then she sat up straight as an arrow and closed her eyes. "I'm ready now."

"Ready for what?" said Mili, blinking.

"My surprise," said Emma.

"What surprise?" asked Mili.

"The one you were planning for me yesterday, when you were out."

Mili looked confused. Emma felt surprised, but not in the way she was expecting. Mili cocked her head to one side. "That's not what I was doing."

Emma felt another sinking feeling coming on.

"I was having *me* time," said Mili.

"What is that?" asked Emma blankly.

Mili looked her right in the eye. "It's time to myself."

Emma thought of her long, lonely afternoon and frowned. "Why would you want to be by *yourself*?"

"It's something I like to do," said Mili. "Sometimes I put on my headphones, listen to polka music, and dance around the room. Yesterday I read a book about snorkeling, baked banana muffins, and made a list of all the people I wanted to visit."

Emma was quiet for a minute.

"May I see your list?" she asked.

Mili walked over to the counter, picked up a piece of paper, and handed it to Emma. At the top, it read, *Go to Emma's apartment and tell her you're glad she is your new neighbor.*

Emma brightened. This was the kind of surprise she had been hoping for. The serious feeling was gone.

"I'm sorry I didn't answer the door when you came," said Mili. "I was so busy with *me* time, I didn't notice *you* knocking."

"Do you think you might be finished with it now?" Emma asked, putting the list down on the table.

Mili nodded. "I am. Do you like polka?"

"I do!" cried Emma, jumping up from her seat.

Mili turned on the radio. When the music came on, around they went, arm in arm, like a helicopter seed spinning out of a maple tree.

CHAPTER 3

The Decision

It was Saturday and Fernando was late, as usual. He grabbed his sweatshirt, put on his sneakers, and ran out the door. Down the stairs he flew, then into the backyard. His neighbors were sitting around the picnic table for 24 Sprout Street's weekly meeting.

Henry stood at the head of the table, looking squarely at Mili. "Since this is your first meeting," he began, "I'll explain how they work." Henry rocked back and forth from his toes to his heels, and lifted his chin into the air. "First, someone raises their paw—"

"Ahem!" coughed Violet.

"Excuse me," Henry continued, "someone raises their paw or their *wing* and brings up a problem. Then we brainstorm ideas to solve it and write them on the board." Henry pointed at a tall chalkboard propped against a tree. "Next, we vote on the best one, and the answer with the most votes wins."

Mili nodded solemnly, and Henry seemed pleased. Henry sat down next to Wilbur. Fernando squeezed in next to Henry.

"What do we have to discuss today?" asked Wilbur.

Violet raised her wing. "The paint on our building is starting to peel. I think it is time to repaint."

Mili raised her paw next, eager to join in. "How about we paint it sunshine yellow?"

"Write it on the board," chirped Violet.

Mili walked over to the chalkboard and wrote, *Sunshine yellow*, then went back to her seat.

Henry frowned. He cleared his throat and stood up again. "I like 24 Sprout Street the way it is," he said, "a nice moss green." He walked to the chalkboard and wrote, *Moss green*.

"Let's vote!" cried Emma, clapping her paws excitedly. She loved a good contest.

"All for moss green," bellowed Henry, raising his paw. He turned to Wilbur and gave him a stern look. Wilbur shifted in his seat, then raised his paw, too.

"All for sunshine yellow," sang Emma. Mili and Emma raised their paws, and Violet raised her wing.

"Fernando," whispered Violet, "you didn't vote."

Fernando had never thought much about the color of 24 Sprout Street. Sunshine yellow

sounded nice. But so did a fresh coat of moss green. "I don't know which to choose," said Fernando. He looked at Henry, who glared back at him. Then he looked at Mili, who smiled a sunshine-yellow smile in his direction.

"It's easy," said Mili. "Just pick the color you like the best."

Fernando smiled back at her and took a breath. Henry stepped in closer and furrowed his brow. Fernando stopped smiling.

"I don't like either one the best," said Fernando. "I like them both the same."

Henry sighed. "You have to choose, Fernando."

"Can I think about it?" he asked.

"Okay by me," declared Emma, hopping up from the table. "I'm late to tai chi!" Emma picked up her bag and skipped down the sidewalk toward Maple Street. The meeting was over.

Henry looked at Fernando. "We'll meet again tomorrow," said Henry. "Try to figure it out by then." He spun around and went inside.

Fernando sat at the table with Mili, Violet, and Wilbur, who was nibbling on a bowl of cashew nuts.

"Maybe you should make a pros-and-cons list," said Mili, taking out her notebook and handing it to him. "First, you write *pros* on one side of the paper. That's where you write all the things you like about a decision. Then you write *cons* on the other side. That's where you put the things you don't like. Then you see which list is longer."

Mili patted Fernando on the back. Then she stood with Violet and Wilbur to go for a walk.

Fernando sat up straight and took out a pen. Under *pro* for sunshine yellow, he wrote, *Mili will be happy with me.* Under *con*, he wrote, *Henry will be angry with me.* Under *pro*, he wrote, *New.* Under *con*, he wrote, *Different.* This was turning out to be trickier than he'd expected.

Next, he made lists for moss green. Under *pro*, he wrote, *Henry will be pleased,* and under *con*, he wrote, *Mili will be disappointed.* He sighed and put the notebook in his sweatshirt pocket.

Fernando returned to his apartment and put on some music. It drifted through the air and lifted his mood. He did three pirouettes around the living room rug, landing in a dining room chair. He looked out the window and thought for a while. Outside, the yellow sunshine played on the moss-green leaves.

There was a knock at the door.

Before Fernando could get up, Henry burst through. "Fernando!" cried Henry, bounding into the living room.

Fernando jumped to standing. "Hi, Henry," he said.

"I was just thinking," began Henry, a little too loudly, "we don't spend enough time together. Can I treat you to an ice cream at Sergio's?"

"Okay," said Fernando, following Henry out the door.

They crossed the yard and headed up Sprout Street. Suddenly Henry grabbed Fernando's arm and pulled him to a stop. "Look at the sage in that hanging basket!" he cried, pointing at a house across the street. "Such a lovely shade of green, isn't it?"

"Sure," said Fernando with
a shrug. He lifted his foot to
keep walking, but Henry held
on to his arm. "And that juniper tree over there!
Such a soothing color, don't you think?"

"I guess," Fernando replied. "Could
we go get some ice cream now?"

"Of course!" cried Henry, letting go
of Fernando's arm and marching ahead.
Fernando hurried to catch up.

When they got to Sergio's, Henry
ordered pistachio for himself and mint
chocolate chip for Fernando. "You
don't mind, do you?" he asked.

"Well, no," said Fernando, wishing he could
have had chocolate mud pie instead.

"Good," said Henry. He handed Fernando

his cone, and they headed back to 24 Sprout Street. This time, Henry didn't stop to admire anything. They just ate their ice cream and walked quietly home.

Fernando returned to his apartment and took out the notebook. He added *Henry will leave me alone* to the pros list for choosing moss green.

He began to think about his new neighbor. "If I voted for sunshine yellow," he thought, "I would make a good impression. Mili would think I was a cheerful sort of guy." Under *pro* for sunshine yellow, Fernando wrote, *Good impression.*

"On the other hand, if I don't vote for moss green, Henry will think I am a bad friend. I've been friends with Henry for a long time." Under *con* for sunshine yellow, Fernando wrote, *Bad friend*. This was not making his decision any easier.

The next morning, Fernando got up early and went into the yard. He crossed the lawn and climbed onto a low branch of the oak tree, where he could get a good look at 24 Sprout Street. He studied the red roof tiles and the porch swing. He could see where the peeling moss-green paint left little chips in the grass near the blueberry bushes.

He glanced over at Henry's window. Inside, Henry was bent over his writing desk. Then he looked up at the second floor. Mili was working on a painting. He thought he could make out the image of a small yellow sunflower on the canvas. He looked down at Henry's apartment again. But now the window was empty.

"Hello up there!" a voice shouted.

Fernando jumped so high, he nearly fell out of the tree. He looked down at Henry.

"Lovely day outside," Henry began, and took a breath.

"I know what you are going to say," said Fernando, stopping him. "The leaves are a beautiful shade of green."

Henry paused. He looked at Fernando, who gazed at his shoes. Then he put his paws in his pockets and lowered his head. "I'm sorry, Fernando," he said. "You should vote for what you like better. Voting for moss green would only make it a tie anyway. Then we'd have to flip a coin."

"That's true," said Fernando.

Henry turned to go, then looked over his shoulder. "I'm going to get cookies for our meeting. What kind would you like?"

Fernando looked up. "Oatmeal raisin, please."

Henry nodded. "Oatmeal raisin it is." And he headed off down the street.

Fernando returned to his apartment and paced back and forth. He thought for a long time. Then he opened Mili's notebook and wrote, under *pro* for moss green, *Henry will know I forgive him.* At last, he knew what to do.

Just then, Fernando caught a glimpse of the clock. "I'm late!" he cried, jumping up and running out the door. Everyone was sitting around the picnic table.

Henry was at the end, putting cookies on a plate.

Fernando sat down. But before he could say anything, Henry stood up. "I would like to change my vote," he said.

Mili gasped. Wilbur's jaw dropped. Emma slapped the table with her paws.

"But moss green was your idea!" cried Violet.

"I know," said Henry, "but I think it's time for a change." He winked at Fernando.

"Let's have a revote!" shouted Emma.

"All for sunshine yellow!" called Violet.

Mili, Henry, Emma, Wilbur, and Violet raised their paws and wing. Fernando breathed a sigh of relief and raised his paw, too. Henry smiled and said, "So we all agree." Then he walked over to where Fernando sat and held out the plate of cookies. Fernando picked one up and happily took a bite.

CHAPTER 4

A Ship Sets Sail

Henry reached into his desk drawer and took out a magnifying glass. He held it up to his eye and leaned forward. "Just as I thought," he said out loud. He put the magnifying glass back in his pocket and picked up a small wooden post. Covering one end with glue, he placed it on the deck of a tiny wooden ship.

"That's better," he said to himself, sitting back to admire it. Henry hadn't been building boats for long, but he felt he had a special talent for it.

He picked up a tiny mouse figurine and placed it carefully at the ship's helm. Lifting the ship into the air, he moved it up and down as though it was bobbing along on the ocean. Henry imagined the waves crashing against its sides and the wind blowing the sail into a wide pillow. "One day, I should sail a ship so handsome," he thought.

He walked over to the counter to set it down to dry. Halfway there, the post rolled off the edge of the deck, then fell, *tik-tik*, onto the floor. He picked it up and looked at it closely. "Broken," he sighed, "and I don't have any more pieces this size. I'll have to go out for more supplies."

He put his ship down and went outside. The leaves above him shifted in the breeze, sending

acorns bouncing onto the ground ahead of him.
He stepped over them and headed up Sprout
Street to Maple, then turned left onto Elm. Two
blocks later, he opened the door to True Blue
Hardware.

"Morning, Henry," said Mr. Ashby behind
the counter.

"Morning," said Henry with a nod, heading to the model-ships aisle. He walked back
and forth, looking for the piece he needed. He
looked up and he looked down. Then his eyes

rested on a post in front of him.

"Aha!" he cried. He reached for the post.
When he had it in his paw, his eyes wan-
dered over to a crack in the display. There
was someone moving behind it.
And that someone looked familiar.

Henry walked to the end of the

aisle and leaned around the corner. Behind the display stood Mili, balancing on her tiptoes and reaching for a small paintbrush above her head.

"Let me!" he called, striding toward her. He climbed up a small shelf, picked up the brush, then handed it to her.

"Thank you," said Mili.

Henry beamed. "What are you painting?" he asked.

"My kitchen cabinets," replied Mili. "My apartment needs a bit of color."

Henry cleared his throat. "I am here for spare parts," he said, puffing out his chest. "I am working on my ship."

"Oh!" Mili cried, lighting up. "There is nothing I like better than floating out on the open sea." She lifted her nose toward an imaginary horizon in the distance, as if she was staring at a great ocean.

Henry nodded, slouching a little. He had never been floating out on the open sea. Henry had never been much of anywhere.

They walked to the register and paid Mr. Ashby for the post and the brush. Then the two headed back to 24 Sprout Street.

"When I lived in Hawaii," said Mili, "sometimes I woke up before dawn and paddled

into deep waters to watch the sun rise, just me and my boat. It was magical."

Henry preferred to sleep in. He had never been up early enough to see the sun rise. And certainly not in a boat. But he couldn't tell Mili that. "I know just what you mean," he said, waving his arm toward the sky. He said it with such certainty, he almost believed it himself.

Mili stopped and turned to Henry. Her eyes were as wide and bright as the sea itself. "I would love to go sailing in your boat," she burst

out. "Let's watch the sun rise tomorrow!"

It took Henry a moment to understand what Mili was asking. His stomach tied itself into a rope knot. He couldn't bear to disappoint her. Henry swallowed and whispered, "Okay."

By the time they arrived back at 24 Sprout Street, a plan was in motion. They would meet on the porch before sunrise to walk to the dock. They would bring raincoats in case of bad weather. Mili would make sandwiches.

"See you tomorrow!" called Mili as she went upstairs.

"Can't wait," squeaked Henry.

He went inside his apartment and sat down in front of his ship. The only creature that could possibly sail it was an ant. If Mili tried to climb inside, it would crumble into a million pieces. Henry had made a terrible mistake.

He racked his brain for a reason to cancel.

Would she believe he had the flu or that his aunt Doris had dropped by? Then finally, he had it.

Henry climbed up the stairs to the second floor and knocked on Mili's door. Violet answered. "Hello, Violet. Is Mili home?"

Mili rushed to the door and beamed at Henry. "I was just telling Violet about tomorrow," said Mili.

"I didn't realize you had a boat!" said Violet.

"That's why I've come by," began Henry. "I am really in no condition to go sailing tomorrow. I've stubbed my toe badly and can barely walk." Henry took a few steps to demonstrate. He limped dramatically from his right foot to his left.

"How terrible!" Violet gasped.

"I have just the thing!" cried Mili, opening her hallway closet and digging through some boxes.

Pot holders and a dustpan went flying over her shoulder. At last, she came out carrying a set of crutches. "Here you go, Henry! Give these a try. You'll be good as new in no time."

"Thank you," said Henry with a frown. He took the crutches and tottered back to his apartment.

He set the crutches by the door and walked over to his ship once more. Too bad it couldn't take them anywhere. He picked it up and set it on the sill by the window. Outside, the wind blew leaves across the yard.

There was a knock at the door. Henry opened it to find Mili on the other side.

"I brought you a bowl of soup for lunch," said Mili, "so that you can stay off your foot."

"Thank you," said Henry, looking at the floor. He carried the bowl to his dining room table.

Mili followed him. "You're not limping any-more," she cried. "It's a miracle!"

Henry froze. His cheeks got hot. He had forgotten to limp, and the crutches were across the room. "Um—yes," coughed Henry, "those crutches really did the trick."

"I'll see you bright and early, then!" Mili bounded out of the room, closing the door behind her.

Henry sat down. It would seem that there was no getting out of his promise.

He tossed and turned late into the night, dreading the ring of his alarm clock. When it finally came, he was already awake. Henry got dressed and went to the front porch to wait.

When Mili came down, she was wearing a shiny red raincoat and her galoshes. In her paw was a canvas bag filled with peanut butter and jelly sandwiches.

"Good morning, neighbor!" she chimed. "I could barely sleep, I was so excited about today."

He put his head in his paws and muttered under his breath, *"Mmppfm."*

"What was that?" asked Mili.

"*Mfphmm,*" said Henry.

Mili furrowed her brow. "I can't understand a word you're saying."

Henry lifted his head and dropped his paws into his lap. "The boat I was telling you about, it is sitting in my window." He sighed and pointed at the sill.

Mili looked through the glass. She could see the silhouette of the tiny vessel resting proudly on the sill. Then she looked at Henry, who couldn't look her in the eye.

"Well," she said at last, "let's take it out."

Henry frowned. "What do you mean? It isn't big enough to carry anyone. It probably doesn't even float."

"Come on," Mili said, waving him inside.

They walked into Henry's apartment and got the ship. Then Mili led him up the steps to the roof. She set the boat on the ledge and found a picnic blanket to spread on the ground beneath it. She put down her bag and unpacked the sandwiches.

From where they sat, it looked as if the boat was resting on quiet water, floating peacefully in the dark. As the sun began to rise up over the buildings on Sprout Street, its rays burst through the trees, casting long shadows across the yard. Henry held his breath.

When the light reached the ship at last, it lit the sails like a lantern. Soon the entire roof was on fire with the electric yellow light. The boat stood there, regal and aglow, against the big sky.

Henry was quiet. Mili was quiet, too.

Then Henry took a bite of his sandwich. "I've never been on a boat," he admitted, "but I think I know what it feels like to sail out over the water at daybreak. You feel big and small at the same time. Like you're the only one left in the world."

"Yes," said Mili, "just you and your boat."

"Just you and your boat and a friend," added Henry.

"Exactly," said Mili.

CHAPTER 5

The Fortune

Wilbur sat at a table for one in Arlene's Chinese Garden. Every Friday, he treated himself to lunch at Arlene's. He liked to relax over a plate of good-luck tofu and gaze out the window at the people walking by.

When he was done with his meal, the waitress brought him the check and a fortune cookie on a little black tray. Wilbur cracked the cookie and pulled the tiny paper fortune from the center. He held it in front of his nose and read it out loud:

"Something wonderful will happen today."

Wilbur popped a piece of cookie into his mouth. He put the fortune in his pocket, placed some money on the table, and waved goodbye to Arlene.

Outside, his bicycle waited. He unlocked it and climbed onto the seat. Something wonderful seemed just around the corner.

Wilbur watched his friends and neighbors bustle down Elm Street, ringing his bell at them as he passed. Mr. Ashby nodded through the window at the hardware store. *Ca-ling!* went Wilbur's bell. When he turned onto Maple Street, Ms. Thornbush waved from Edie's coffee shop. *Ca-ling!*

As Wilbur got closer to Sergio's, he could see a crowd gathering outside. On Friday, Sergio baked fresh bread, and a long line of customers waited to buy it. At the end of the line was a familiar face.

"Afternoon, neighbor!" Henry said, waving. Next to him was his cousin Theodore. "Notice anything different?" Henry put his paws on his hips and stepped forward.

Wilbur slowed his bike to a stop and rested his foot on the sidewalk. He looked Henry up and down. On his feet were a pair of brand-new green suede loafers with a penny in the top.

"Aren't they elegant?" Henry beamed. "Theodore bought them for me this morning. They were on sale at Emerson's Shoe Galleria. And they match my wool blazer!"

"Wonderful," Wilbur offered, giving Henry a pat on the arm. He thought about how nice it would be to have someone buy him a new pair of shoes. Then he reached in his pocket and felt for the fortune. Pushing off the sidewalk, he continued down the street.

As he approached the New Valley Theater, something caught his eye. Outside was a large marquee that read *It Takes Two to Tango*. Underneath was a poster of a dog and a cat dancing together under a streetlight. He slowed down to take a closer look.

Ca-link-a-link! The front door swung wide, and people streamed out in a cloud of chatter into the bright sun. Two of those people were Violet and Fernando, walking arm in arm, laughing and swinging their jackets.

"Hi, Wilbur!" they called out together.

"You would not believe the play we just saw," cheered Violet.

"Full of dancing!" cried Fernando. "And the costumes! It was like we traveled around the world and back."

"*We'll always have New York!*" sang Violet. Then they both burst into laughter.

Wilbur didn't get the joke. "Wonderful," he said, rubbing his toe on the sidewalk. Though he was beginning to feel a little less wonderful himself. He wondered if he might be the only one spending the day by himself.

Violet and Fernando went to get ice cream, and Wilbur headed home. He pulled up to 24 Sprout Street to find Emma standing with her tai chi class in the yard. They were moving their arms slowly up and down. It looked as

though they were dancing to a tune he couldn't hear.

"Howdy, Wilbur!" shouted Emma from across the lawn.

Wilbur waved, then decided to keep going.

"Wait, I have something to tell you!" she called.

Wilbur pretended not to hear. He was not in the mood to learn about the wonderful time his friends were having. Instead, he pedaled down Sprout Street, lost in thought.

He reached the bottom of the street and turned left onto Cedar Hill Road. As he climbed up the hill, he had to stand to push the pedals down. His breath sped up as the bike slowed. He held the handlebars tightly.

At last, the hill became too steep to climb. Wilbur slowed to a stop and got off his bike. He tried to catch his breath. His feet hurt and his legs ached. It did not seem to be such a wonderful day after all. He reached into his pocket for his fortune.

But it wasn't there. Wilbur reached inside again, feeling around, then tried his back pocket to be sure. The little slip of paper was gone.

SWISH! Just then, a bike whirred down the hill at top speed. The gust sent fur flying into the air and Wilbur backward onto the ground.

The other biker screeched to a stop. She looked over her shoulder, shading her eyes from the sun.

"Wilbur?"

"Hello, Mili," Wilbur said with a nod. He stood up slowly, his legs shaky.

"Wilbur!" Mili cried as she pushed her bike back up the hill. "I'm so sorry, I didn't see you there! Are you okay?"

"Yes, I think so," sighed Wilbur.

"What were you doing on the side of the road?" she asked.

"I was looking for the fortune from my cookie," said Wilbur. "I seem to have lost it."

"Then I will help you find it!" said Mili.

"All right," said Wilbur.

Mili hopped back on her bike. "Let's retrace your steps."

They turned around together and coasted

down the hill, watching the sidewalk for the missing fortune.

"Where were you last?" she asked as they reached the bottom.

"I came from Maple Street," he replied.

So the two made their way up Sprout Street, toward Maple. Mili began to sway back and forth on her bike. "Let's play I Spy!" she called out. "It will help us find what we're looking for."

Wilbur didn't see how that would help, but he was fond of the game. And he was glad to play it with Mili. "Okay," said Wilbur. "I spy the oak tree."

Mili looked over at the tree in front of 24 Sprout Street.

Beneath it stood Emma, moving her arms like a bird flapping its wings. "I spy a pigeon," teased Mili. Wilbur looked at Emma and chuckled.

On the corner of Sprout and Maple stood Henry and Theodore, each holding an armful of baguettes. Wilbur looked at Mili. "I spy my afternoon snack!" said Wilbur. This time, Mili laughed.

As they got closer, Wilbur held out his paw. Henry saw him and nodded, holding out a loaf.

"Thank you!" called Wilbur, snatching it up as they zoomed past. He broke it in half and gave a piece to Mili.

They continued up Maple Street, snacking on the baguette. Soon Violet and Fernando were walking toward them, eating ice cream cones. "I spy dessert," Mili said with a grin.

"Great minds think alike!" said Wilbur. This time, they stopped, parked their bikes in front of Sergio's, and got two cones to go.

Back outside, Mili took a bite of her cone. Then she turned to Wilbur. "Do you want to keep looking for your fortune?" she asked.

"That's okay," said Wilbur. "I don't think I need it anymore."

By the time they got back to Sprout Street, the two were laughing like old friends. They climbed down from their bikes and rested them against the porch, then sat down to finish their cones.

"Wilbur!" shouted Emma, running toward them across the yard. "You dropped something before!" She reached into her pocket and pulled out the fortune, placing it by his feet.

"You found it!" cried Mili.

Wilbur picked it up and read it out loud. "Something wonderful will happen today."

"Well, did it come true?" asked Emma.

"Yes," Wilbur said, looking at Mili, "I think it did."

CHAPTER 6

Happy New Year

Mili walked into her living room and set a box down on the sofa. It was the last one to unpack. She had been putting things away in her new home for months, and her apartment felt cozy and full.

She reached for a pair of scissors and cut the tape on the top of the box. As she pulled it open, Mili thought of the day she'd left her island home, far, far away.

The sun had beamed down on her shoulders

as she flip-flopped down the sidewalk. The bus to the airport waited at the curb. It was February, but sunny and warm. A soft breeze blew the leaves of the palm trees that lined the street.

It had taken three weeks to pack up all her things and ship them over a wide ocean and across the country to her new home. When the boxes were gone and her apartment was empty, her neighbors came over to say goodbye. They sat on overturned baskets, ate sliced pineapple, and danced under strings of jasmine flowers.

Mili reached into the box and pulled out a red

tin wrapped in twine. She tugged the string and opened the creaky top. Inside was a stack of photos. On the top was a picture of Mili surrounded by her old friends. She was wearing a lei around her neck and smiling. On the back, it said, "Bon voyage!" and "We'll miss you!" and *"A hui hou!"*

Suddenly Mili's apartment wasn't feeling so cozy. It felt cold and empty. Outside, snowflakes fell from a gray sky, making the yard look like the moon. Mili shivered.

She put the photo on her fridge with a magnet. Then she pulled the door open to get a slice of cheese. But her refrigerator was empty.

Mili picked up a shopping bag and walked to her closet. Inside was a thick alpaca sweater. She pulled it over her head. Looking out the window at the sea of snowflakes, she shivered again. "Surely I will freeze with just one sweater," she thought. So out came a second, which she wrapped around the first. On top she layered a puffy green vest, zipping it tightly over the sweaters.

Waddling to the coat rack, Mili squeezed a thick, fleece-trimmed parka on top of the rest. Around her neck she wrapped a long wool scarf, and finished it all off with a hat knit by her cousin Betsy, two pairs of earmuffs, and some mittens. Mili looked like a small mountain.

She wobbled down the stairway, one step at a time, holding the railing so as not to lose her bal-

ance. She was not used to moving underneath so many layers of clothes. At last, she arrived at the front door.

Mili waddled into the cold. As she reached to close the door behind

her, a gust of wind knocked her to the floor of
the porch, and she rolled back inside like a bil-
liard ball. Mili pulled herself up. This time, she
fought the wind with all her might and forced
the door shut.

Two figures moved back and forth in the
yard. Next to them was a small mound of snow.
When the wind died down, Mili made her way
toward them.

"Happy New Year!"
shouted Wilbur as she
got closer. He was pat-
ting a handful of snow
on the snow mound. His
cheeks were rosy, and his
breath made little clouds in the air.

"Is that Mili under there?" asked Violet. She
put down the snowball she was rolling and

squinted in Mili's direction. "Happy New Year!" she said at last. "Are you coming to my party tonight?"

"Yes, I think so," said Mili, adjusting her earmuffs. "What are you making?"

"A snow cat!" answered Wilbur with a grin.

"Care to join us?" added Violet.

"No thanks," said Mili. "I have to go get groceries. Besides, I wouldn't know how. We don't have snow like this in Hawaii." Mili threw her scarf over her shoulder and turned to go.

She made her way across the yard and down the snowy sidewalk toward Maple Street. She lifted each foot high into the air, then dropped it, *ka-PLUSH,* into the snow ahead. A wobbly trail of footprints spread out behind her, as though a coconut had bounced down the hill.

By the time she made it to Sergio's, she was huffing and puffing like a steam train. She exhaled little cotton puffs into the great, snowy sky. She stopped to rest.

Above the entrance was a hand-painted sign that read *Have a Happy New Year!* Mili watched it shift back and forth in the icy wind. She reached for the door. *SPLUSH!* A little well of snow that had collected on the sign fell smack on top of her head. It slid slowly down her back and, *kush,* onto the ground. She was starting to think it would not be such a happy new year.

Inside, the store was full of bundled shoppers filling their carts and leaving snowy trails behind them. Mili walked to the bread aisle and chose a loaf of cinnamon raisin. The chill from outside faded, and it began to heat up inside Mili's sweaters. She started to roast.

Fanning her face with her shopping list, she bobbed toward the produce section. She had to step very carefully over the slushy pools at her feet.

"Hi, Mili!" cried a voice from behind her. She whipped around to see who it was. *Thwish!* Her foot sailed through a puddle, then flew straight up into the air. Mili lay in a soggy pile on the floor.

"Are you okay?" asked Emma, running over.

"I think so," said Mili, her cheeks turning pink. "It's just that I'm not used to dressing like this. In Hawaii, I wore a sundress all year round."

"I would like that very much," said Emma. "I don't care for the snow." Emma was stuffed into a parka that reached her ankles and wrapped in a scarf that covered her face up to the nose.

She helped Mili back to her feet, and they shuffled to the register together. Sergio rang them up. Emma took her bag and went to chat with Ms. Bunkerstein by the deli. Mili took

hers and headed out the door. It was a world of white.

Mili walked and walked, swinging back and forth on the sidewalk like the pendulum of a clock. Her fingers began to tingle, and little beads of ice formed on her scarf. "I must be close to Sprout Street by now," she thought. But the street sign wasn't anywhere to be seen.

Ahead of her was a frozen pond filled with ice skaters. Had she walked all the way to the

park? She slowed her pace and turned to go when someone called her name.

"Mili!" cried a skater gliding toward her, dressed in a plaid snowsuit. Mili put her mittened paw over her brow to block the falling snow. She narrowed her eyes. Fernando flew toward her. "Happy New Year, Mili! Are you here to skate?"

"I don't know how," said Mili. "Can you tell me how to get back to 24 Sprout Street? I seem to have lost my way."

"Sure thing," said Fernando. "Just turn around and follow your footprints back to the hedge at the next block. Then go left."

"Thanks," said Mili, turning to go.

"Will I see you tonight?" called Fernando.

"Maybe," shouted Mili over her shoulder.

She tried to find her footprints, but all she could see was a soft white blanket covering the sidewalk. Mili walked on, looking for the hedge.

The more she walked, the heavier her clothes became. At the top of a hill, she set her bag in the snow and sat down to rest. The sun hung low on the horizon. She began to worry. "What if I never find my way home?"

Mili stood up again and reached for her bag. But it wasn't there. Looking ahead, she saw it sliding down the icy hill. Mili lunged, but her feet were not steady on the ice below. *THWISH!* She sailed down the hill after the bag.

Snowflakes flew past her face like falling stars. Buildings reached into the sky above her,

 whirring past like bowling pins knocked loose by a high-speed bowling ball.

SMACK! Mili hit something hard, then stopped sliding. She pressed her mittens into the ground and pushed herself to standing. A small gray nose poked out of a pile of snow at her feet.

"Happy New Year to you, too," said Henry.

"Henry! Are you okay?" Mili found his paw in the snowbank and helped him up.

"Yes," said Henry. "This isn't my first tumble."

"I'm so sorry," Mili went on. "In Hawaii, the sidewalks are never covered in ice."

"It sounds lovely there," said Henry, dusting off the snow.

Mili looked over Henry's shoulder and realized they were standing right in front of 24

Sprout Street. Then she looked at the ground. Her bag lay in a snowdrift, with her groceries sprinkled around it. Henry helped her gather them up, then walked her inside.

Mili returned to her apartment. It had been a long day and her head hung heavy. She took off her soggy clothes, put away her groceries, and drew a hot, steamy bath. She sat in the water until she felt as warm as a sea lion lying on a sandy beach. Then she got up and put on her robe.

Settling into her reading chair, she picked up a book about sailing and let her mind float away. Before she knew it, the sky was dark behind her windows and the clock struck eight. Violet's party was about to begin. But Mili didn't feel like going. Maybe it was better to start this new year at home, where she was safe and snug. She turned up the heat and went into the kitchen for some tea.

On her way, she passed the photo on the fridge. Her old friends were gathered around her by the ocean. The sun was setting behind them, sending brilliant orange-and-red sunbeams across the clouds. Their faces glowed with happiness.

Mili thought of Violet, Emma, Fernando, Henry, and Wilbur. There might not have been any sunshine outside, but there was plenty inside 24

Sprout Street. Suddenly she felt warm all over. So she walked to her closet and put on a party dress.

Mili knocked on Violet's door. Giggles spilled out from behind it. "Come in!" someone called.

Mili opened the door and gasped. A vase full of purple orchids sat on an orange-striped tablecloth. Mango and macadamia nuts were arranged in little dishes around it. Ukulele music floated through the air while Wilbur and Emma danced the hula in a corner.

Violet walked over and put a lei around

her neck. "Happy New Year!" she cried. "We thought we would ring in the New Year in Hawaiian style."

Mili melted. She popped a piece of mango in her mouth and spun around to the music. She stepped and swayed late into the night. And as each hour passed, she was more and more certain it would be a very happy new year after all.

SPROUT STREET
NEIGHBORS

"This book has the heart of Winnie-the-Pooh and the charm of Frog and Toad. Can I move in next door?" —Grace Lin, Newbery Honor author

SPROUT STREET
NEIGHBORS
Five Stories

ANNA ALTER

Illustration © 2015 by Anna Alter.

Read more about the charming animal friends
who live at 24 Sprout Street!

RandomHouseKids.com